George Brown, CLASS CLOWN

A Royal Pain in the Burp

For Ian and Mandy
(young branches on an old family tree!)—NK

For Mr. OB and other inspiring teachers—AB

GROSSET & DUNLAP
Published by the Penguin Group
Penguin Group (USA) LLC, 375 Hudson Street, New York, New York 10014 USA

USA | Canada | UK | Ireland | Australia | New Zealand | India | South Africa | China

penguin.com
A Penguin Random House Company

Library of Congress Cataloging-in-Publication Data is available.

ISBN 978-0-448-48283-5   10 9 8 7 6 5 4 3 2 1

George Brown,
CLASS CLOWN
A Royal
Pain in the
Burp

by Nancy Krulik
illustrated by Aaron Blecha

Grosset & Dunlap
An Imprint of Penguin Group (USA) LLC

Chapter 1

"I want everyone to enjoy a big piece of my Monday-morning surprise," Mrs. Kelly told the fourth-graders as she put plates on each of their desks. "It's **monkey bread**! And it's delicious."

George Brown had never seen anything like this. It did not look delicious. It looked **lumpy and brown**.

"Is this bread made from monkeys?" George asked nervously.

Everyone in the class started laughing.

"No," Mrs. Kelly assured him. "It's made from flour, cinnamon, and sugar. Many people bake monkey bread, but this is my grandmother's special recipe."

"Why is it called monkey bread?" George asked.

"I don't really know," Mrs. Kelly admitted. "But some people say monkey bread got its name because it resembles the bark of the **monkey puzzle tree**."

"What's a monkey puzzle?" Max asked. "Is that like a jigsaw puzzle?"

Mrs. Kelly walked over to her computer and posted a picture on the smart board.

"This is a monkey puzzle tree," Mrs. Kelly said, pointing to the picture of a tall evergreen tree with grayish-brown bark.

George looked at the picture. The tree didn't look very much like the **brown lump** on the plate in front of him.

"Monkey bread's delicious, dude," said George's friend Alex. "Try it."

George wasn't sure. But Alex had

never lied to him. So George picked off a piece and took a bite.

"Mmmm . . . ," George said. **"That *is* good."**

"Told ya," Alex replied. He took a big bite of his monkey bread.

"This has raisins in it," Sage said. "I've never had monkey bread with raisins before."

"That's how my grandmother made it in the bakery she ran," Mrs. Kelly explained.

"Wow, I wish *my* grandmother ran a bakery," George said. "Then I could get **free cookies and cakes** all the time."

"I did," Mrs. Kelly said. "I was very lucky. Growing up, many of my relatives were in the food business. Like my great-uncle Edgar. He ran an ostrich farm. So I got free **ostrich eggs**. Those eggs were huge. You could make an omelet that would feed three people with . . ."

George wanted to pay attention to what his teacher was saying. He really did. But he couldn't. He was too focused on what his *belly* was saying.

Bing-bong. Ping-pong.

George's tummy was making all kinds of noises. It was **full of bubbles**. Not just any kind of bubbles. Strong, crazy bubbles. The kind of bubbles that slam-danced against his stomach and boomeranged off his bladder.

Bubbles that could cause a lot of trouble if they burst out of him.

George had to keep himself from burping. Because if the burp got loose, there was no telling what **horrible** thing it would make him do. After all, the burp had gotten him in trouble plenty of times before.

It all started when George and his family had moved to Beaver Brook. George's dad was in the army, and his family moved around a lot. So George knew that first days at school could be **pretty rotten**. But *this* first day was the rottenest.

In his old school, George had been the class clown. But George had promised himself that things were going to be different at Edith B. Sugarman Elementary School. No more pranks. No more **goofing on teachers** when their backs were turned.

Unfortunately, no one at George's new school even noticed the non-funny new kid. They acted like he was **invisible**.

That night, George's parents took him out to Ernie's Ice Cream Emporium. While they were sitting outside and George was finishing his root beer float, a shooting star flashed across the sky. **So George made a wish.**

I want to make kids laugh—but not get into trouble.

Unfortunately, the star was gone before George could finish the wish. So only half came true—the first half.

A minute later, George had a **funny feeling** in his belly. It was like there were hundreds of tiny bubbles bouncing around in there. The bubbles ping-ponged their way into his chest, and bing-bonged their way up into his throat. And then . . .

George let out a big burp. A *huge* burp. A SUPER burp!

The super burp was loud, and it was *magic*.

Suddenly George lost control of his arms and legs. It was like they had minds of their own. His hands grabbed straws and **stuck them up his nose**, making him look like a walrus. His feet jumped up on the table and started dancing the hokey pokey. Everyone at Ernie's Emporium started laughing—except George's parents, who were covered in the **ice cream** he'd kicked over while he was dancing.

The burp came back over and over

again. And every time it did, it made **a mess of things**. A mess George got in trouble for. Which was why George couldn't let that burp burst out of him now!

But the burp really wanted to come out and play.

Cling clang! Already the bubbles were kicking at his kidneys and climbing up his colon.

Twing twang! The bubbles twisted around his teeth and tickled his tongue.

And then . . .

Uh-oh! The magical super burp was free. Now whatever the burp wanted to do, George had to do. And what the burp wanted to do was **monkey around**.

His mouth started making monkey

sounds. "Ook, ook, ook!"

His arms started scratching at his fur . . . uh . . . er, *skin.*

His back curved. And his feet started bouncing up and down.

"George is getting all **weird** again!" Louie Farley told Mrs. Kelly.

George frowned. Louie was such a **tattletale**. Not that Mrs. Kelly had to be told. It was hard to miss all that ooking, scratching, and bouncing.

"Ook! Ook!" George said.

His hands stopped scratching just long enough to grab **a big hunk** of monkey bread from Mrs. Kelly's desk. Then he shoved the bread into his mouth.

"George, that's rude!" Mrs. Kelly scolded. "Sit down now!"

George wanted to sit down. He really did. But George wasn't in charge. The burp was. And it wanted to go ape!

"Ook! Ook!"

Scratch, scratch.

Pop!

Just then, George felt something **burst in his belly**. All the air rushed out of him. The super burp was gone. But George was still there, all bent over with his hands scratching his sides.

"Oooh. George is gonna get it now," Louie told his pals, Max and Mike.

Mrs. Kelly sighed. She said, "I know monkey bread is delicious. Especially the first time you try it. But that's **no excuse** for just grabbing it, George."

George sat down and opened his mouth to say "I'm sorry." And that's exactly what came out.

Mrs. Kelly nodded. Then she continued with the lesson. "My grandmother and my great-uncle Edgar were fascinating people. But I'll bet you don't know why I told you about them."

The kids all **stared** at her. They had no idea.

"Everyone has interesting people in their family," Mrs. Kelly explained. "And you're going to learn about *your* relatives when we study our **family trees** in social studies this week."

"Social studies?" Max asked. "Didn't we just study trees in *science*?"

"Family trees aren't real trees," Mrs. Kelly explained. "They're your family history. I want each of you to research your family tree to find someone who did something **unexpected or exciting**."

"What if everyone in our family tree is boring?" George asked.

"I'll bet there's someone in your family who did something

surprising," Mrs. Kelly assured him. "And you're going to get to tell everyone in Beaver Brook about it on Friday night during our **Family Tree Festival Assembly**."

"How are we going to fit everyone from Beaver Brook in the auditorium?" Mike asked.

"We're not," Mrs. Kelly assured him. "Your parents will be invited to come to the assembly. Everyone else can **watch on TV** at home. A reporter from *Channel Forty-Seven News* will be there to film your reports for a special they're doing on family trees."

That got George's attention. TV was a huge deal.

"Wow!" Julianna exclaimed. "That's the news my family watches."

"Mine too," Sage said. "I love the way they make **little frowny faces** on the raindrops during the weather report."

"I'm going to have to get a haircut if I'm going to be on TV," Louie said. "I want to look good."

George snickered. It would take more than a haircut to make Louie look good.

"How are we going to find out about our ancestors?" Alex asked Mrs. Kelly.

"You can start online," Mrs. Kelly explained. "I will show you a website that locates documents that tell you where **your relatives** came from and what jobs they had."

"I don't need a website to tell me my relatives had important jobs that made a lot of money," Louie said. "The Farleys are all important—and rich."

"Don't be so sure," Mrs. Kelly warned Louie. "You never know what you may find out when you look into your history. **Strange branches** can be found on family trees."

"Who knows what kind of strange things are hanging from George's tree," George heard Louie whisper to Max and Mike.

Alex must have heard it, too, because he whispered to George, "Louie's a jerk."

George laughed. "Yeah. They could have named **beef jerky** after the people on the Farley family tree," he whispered back to Alex.

Then he shook his head. That couldn't be right. Because beef jerky was pretty good. And there was **nothing good** about Louie Farley.

Chapter 2

"I don't think my family tree is going to be filled with **important rich people** like Louie says his is," George told Alex and Chris as the boys walked into Chris's bedroom later that afternoon. The boys had decided to start researching their family-tree projects together using Chris's computer.

"You never know," Alex replied. "Where did your family come from?"

George shrugged. "Our last house was in Cherrydale."

"No, I mean where did your family come from *originally*?" Alex explained.

"Before they lived in America."

"I don't know," George admitted.

"I bet we'll find out a lot of **cool things** about our families," Chris said.

George wished he could be as excited as Chris was about this project. But he wasn't. He had a feeling that on Friday night, he would be standing in front of a **whole room of people**, talking about how boring his family was.

"You guys mind if I go first?" Chris asked.

"Go ahead," Alex said.

Chris hurried over to the computer. He went to the website and typed in his name, his birthday, and the place he was born. Then he hit Send and sat back.

A moment later, a list of people with Chris's last name **popped up** on the screen. Chris looked for the names he recognized, like his parents, his grandparents, and his aunt. He put checks next to their names and hit Send again.

Now a **long list** of Chris's relatives popped up on the screen. People he had never heard of, going all the way back to the 1800s! The list showed their birthdates, where they were born, whom they were married to, how many kids they had, and what they did for a living.

"Check it out!" Chris shouted. "I had a great-great-great-grandfather named Larry, who was **a plumber**! That's perfect. I can talk about my great-great-great-grandfather and my Toiletman comic books at the assembly. I might even add a Larry the Plumber character to my newest comic."

George laughed. Chris was so proud of his **Toiletman comic books**. He even had a Toiletman costume, complete with

a plunger sword and a **toilet-seat shield**.
He wore the costume whenever he could—
in the school talent show, to a comic-book
convention, and, of course, on Halloween.
Even though Halloween had been a while
ago, **the costume** was still sitting in the
corner of his room.

Chris pulled out a piece of paper
and started drawing his new character,
Larry the Plumber. Next, Alex sat at the
computer and typed in his information.

"Well, that's interesting," he said finally.

"Do you have a whole lot of scientists in your family?" George asked him. He figured there had to be. After all, Alex was a **science fanatic**. That had to come from somewhere.

"No," Alex said. "But my great-uncle Samuel was a hypnotist."

"A what?" Chris asked.

"**A hypnotist**," Alex repeated. "One of those guys who puts people to sleep and then makes them do things by the power of suggestion."

"I once saw a guy do that on TV," George said. "He made a lady **cluck like a chicken** every time she heard a bell ring. It was hilarious."

"I wonder if I have time to learn how to hypnotize people before Friday," Alex said. "That would make a really cool presentation."

"If anyone can do it, you can," George assured him.

"Okay, George. Your turn," Alex said.

George sat down at the computer and entered his information.

A whole list of relatives came up. George **checked off** the names he recognized, and waited. Then suddenly, his family tree appeared on the screen.

George scanned the list for someone who had done something interesting. There were some family members who were in the military and a few teachers. There was a third cousin once removed who owned **a Laundromat**. Nothing out of the ordinary. Nothing that would be cool to talk about at the assembly.

Suddenly, George saw **something strange** pop up on his list. Something he could never have imagined. His eyes opened wide. He read it again. And again.

That couldn't be right.

"Hey, you guys," he called out. "Does this say what I *think* it says?"

Chris and Alex peered over George's shoulder.

"Whoa!" Alex exclaimed.

"Wow!" Chris added. "You're probably the only kid in the whole grade with a relative like that. Maybe even in the whole school."

"Or the whole town," Alex added. "I mean, it's not like there are that many people who are related to **real live royalty**."

"You think it's right?" George asked.

"Mrs. Kelly gave us the website," Alex told him. "It has to be reliable."

"That means it's true." George gasped. "I'm really related to **His Majesty, King Stanley of Arfendonia**."

"Yup," Alex said. "According to this, you are his seventeenth cousin twice removed on your mother's side."

"Wow!" George said.

"Does that mean you could be king of Arfendonia one day?" Chris asked.

"I don't know," George replied.

"You're pretty far removed," Alex told him. "But it's possible. You have royal **Arfendonian blood** running through your veins, dude."

"Where's Arfendonia?" Chris asked George.

George shook his head. "I have no idea. I never heard of it."

"Me either," Alex admitted. "But we can look it up."

George typed *Arfendonia* into the

search engine. Almost immediately a map came up on the screen. At first, all George saw was a lot of blue water off the coast of northern Europe. But when he zoomed in, he saw a **small black dot** in the middle of the water with the word *Arfendonia* next to it. The word was bigger than the dot.

"Well, now we know where my family comes from," George said.

"What does it say about it?" Chris asked him.

"'Arfendonia,'" George read. "'A **small island** located in the North Atlantic Ocean.'"

"What else does it say?" Chris asked.

"That's it," George told him.

"If you become King George of Arfendonia, will you get to **wear a crown**?" Chris asked George.

"I guess so," George said. "Don't all kings wear crowns?"

"You could probably **knight people**, too," Chris added excitedly.

George reached over and grabbed the plunger from Chris's Toiletman Halloween costume. "Kneel down," he told Chris.

Chris got down on one knee in front of George.

"I dub thee Sir Chris of Arfendonia," George said as he tapped Chris on each shoulder with the plunger.

"Thank you, King George," Chris joked. "You can count on me to **flush** all the bad guys out of Arfendonia."

George laughed. "How about you,

Alex?" he asked. "You wanna be a royal knight of Arfendonia?"

"No, thanks," Alex said. "I don't know where that plunger's been."

"Oh, you don't have to worry about that," Chris said. "It's only been used once, **in an emergency**. And I washed it off really well after."

"Thanks anyway," Alex said. "I have to get home."

"Me too," George added. He grabbed his backpack and his jacket. "I don't want to be late for dinner. My mom's making **tuna casserole** tonight. It doesn't taste so great when it gets cold."

"Is tuna casserole an Arfendonian dish?" Chris asked him.

George shrugged. "I don't know anything about Arfendonia," he admitted.

"After Friday's assembly, everyone will know about it," Alex said. "You're going to be the **biggest news** of the whole program."

George thought Alex could be right. The other kids were going to be so impressed. Well, most of them, anyway. Louie would probably just be mad. He was always **bragging** about how the Farley family was the most powerful and richest in the whole school. Which they probably had been—

Until now!

Chapter 3

"I couldn't believe it," George heard Sage saying as he and Alex walked onto the playground before school the next morning. "I didn't even know **snakes could be milked**. But that's what my second cousin once removed did for a living."

"Why would anyone want snake milk?" Julianna asked.

"I read that they use it to make medicine for people who have snakebites," Sage explained. "It can be used as **antivenom**."

George smiled. Milking snakes was definitely cool. But not as cool as being king of **a whole country**. He opened his mouth to tell everyone about his interesting relative, but Julianna started talking before he could get a word out.

"My great-aunt was an airplane pilot," Julianna said. "I've always wanted to fly. I guess I'm a lot like her."

"It's amazing what you can find out on that website," George began. "My—"

"I'm a lot like my relatives, too," Max interrupted. "I had a few **chimney sweeps** in my family tree."

"How are you like a chimney sweep?" Louie asked him.

"I'm always a mess," Max told him. "My mom says I'm a **dirt magnet**. And chimney sweeps get pretty dirty doing their jobs."

George couldn't wait any longer.

"Wait until you guys hear—" he began.

But Mike started talking right over him. "My great-grandmother was a **potato-chip inspector**," he told everyone. "She made sure the chips were shaped right, and that they had just enough salt on them."

He pulled a potato chip out of his lunch bag and licked the salt off. "Mmm. Perfect," he said as he chomped down on the chip. **Bits of potato chip** flew out of his mouth.

"I could get used to tasting potato chips all day," Julianna said.

George was bursting with excitement. He couldn't hold in his news any longer. **"I'm related to a king!"** he blurted.

Everyone stopped talking.

"You're what?" Julianna asked.

"Related to a king," George repeated. "King Stanley of Arfendonia. He's my seventeenth cousin twice removed on my mother's side."

"Oh, Georgie," Sage **gushed**. She batted her eyelids up and down.

George shook his head. He hated when Sage called him Georgie. What kind of a name was that for royalty? King *Georgie*?

"You're related to a king?" Julianna repeated. **"That's just crazy."**

"I'll say," Louie agreed. "Crazy. Which is what George is. Crazy. As in cuckoo. Nuts. There's no way that **weirdo freak** could ever be a king."

"Actually, there is," Alex said. "A whole lot of people would have to die or turn down their right to be king in order for him to do it, but George could possibly be king of Arfendonia someday."

"The website **has to be wrong**," Louie continued. "Royal families are rich. And George isn't rich. *I* am."

"But are you related to a king?" George asked him.

Louie scowled. "Where is this Arfendonia place, anyway? I've never heard of it. Have any of you guys?"

The kids all shook their heads.

"See?" Louie said. "He's making the

whole thing up. There's no Arfendonia.
And there isn't any king. You need to
come up with something better than this,
George. Otherwise you're going to make
a **fool** of yourself in front of everyone in
Beaver Brook!"

BUZZZZ. At just that moment, the
buzzer rang. It was time for school to
start.

"After you, Your Majesty," Alex said with a grin and a bow.

George tried to force a smile onto his face. **It wasn't easy.** After what Louie said, he wasn't feeling so happy anymore.

Louie was right. Nobody had ever heard of Arfendonia. It was too small. Too far away. And no one—not even George—knew anything about it.

If George didn't come up with some interesting facts about the place soon, he was going to be **royally embarrassed** on Friday night.

Chapter 4

"Ms. Folio," George said to the school librarian later that day, "where are the books on **foreign cultures**?"

"Look in the three hundred section," Ms. Folio told him. "Where the social science books are."

"Thanks," George said. He started to walk over to that section of the library, hoping to find a book there about the people and customs of Arfendonia.

"What are you **staring** at?" Louie demanded as George passed the table where he was sitting. He **slammed his book shut** and threw his body over the cover so George couldn't see it.

"I wasn't staring," George said. "I don't care what you're reading." Although now that Louie had made such a **big stink** about it, George was kind of curious about what he was hiding.

But Louie wasn't giving any clues. He just lay on top of his book until George walked away.

Grrr. Lucky Louie. He probably had **tons of information** on what his relative did and where he or she lived.

Once at the 300 section, George pulled out a book about kingdoms around the world. He looked at the index. There it was: *Arfendonia . . . Page 23.*

Okay, so it was only one page. But a guy could get a lot of information out of one page.

Or maybe not.

The only thing George saw on page twenty-three was a huge picture of grass dotted with **purple flowers**. The caption read: *The island of Arfendonia has many gardens with flowers that bloom in the spring.*

That was it? Flowers in Arfendonia bloomed in the spring? *Duh*. Flowers *everywhere* bloomed in the spring. That **wasn't helpful** at all.

What was George supposed to do on Friday night? Stand there with a crown on his head holding up purple flowers? He'd look like a royal **doofus**!

George looked around the room. Alex was busy taking notes about how to do hypnotism. Julianna had a huge stack of airplane books next to her. Sage was reading about snakes. Mike was **chomping** on a potato chip, which was okay, because it was research.

The only one not doing anything was George.

"Are you okay, George?" Ms. Folio asked him.

George shook his head. "There's

no information in these books about the country my family is from."

"There are other ways to do research, George," Ms. Folio said.

"I already looked on the Internet, and I **couldn't find** anything out," George told her. "My country looked like a dot. I actually thought it was a **speck of dirt** at first."

"Have you talked to any of your relatives?" Ms. Folio asked him. "Maybe **your grandparents** know something about the old country."

George shrugged. "My grandma never mentioned anything about it before."

"Perhaps that's because no one's ever asked," Ms. Folio suggested.

"So you mean I can do research just **by talking**?" George asked. "I don't have to look in a book?"

Ms. Folio nodded. "It's called getting an oral history," she explained. "That's how people learned history before there were books. They told each other **stories** about the past."

George shook his head. It was hard to imagine there was ever a time without books. "I guess it's worth a try," he said finally.

As George put his book back on the

shelf, he heard **Louie laughing**. "What's the matter, George? Can't find your made-up country?"

George didn't answer. What was the point?

"Some king," Louie continued. "You're the king of *nothing*."

Chapter 5

"Wow. I hadn't thought about Arfendonia in years," George's grandma told him as she took a **sip of her tea**. It was Wednesday afternoon. George's mom had driven him to her house after school so he could do some oral-history research.

"Do you know King Stanley?" George asked her.

His grandmother shook her head.

"I don't know anyone in Arfendonia," she admitted. **"I've never been there.** No one from our family has been there since *my* grandmother and grandfather moved here."

George frowned. It didn't seem like his grandmother was going to be much help.

"So you don't even know if we're really related to King Stanley?" George asked sadly.

"Oh, we're probably related," his grandmother assured him. "It's a very small country. Everyone there is related to the **royal family** somehow."

"Didn't your grandparents ever tell you anything about what it was like living in Arfendonia?" George wondered.

"Not really," George's grandma admitted.

Oh brother. This was going nowhere. George was **miserable**.

Which he knew would make Louie really happy.

Which only made George *more* miserable.

"Wait a minute, Mom," George's mother piped up. "Isn't your grandmother's **old trunk** up in the attic?"

George's grandma nodded. "You're right," she said. "There are probably some Arfendonian things in there."

"You think there's anything that could help me with my presentation?" George asked anxiously.

His grandmother shrugged. "I don't know," she said. "But it's worth a look."

As George climbed up the narrow stairs to the attic, he spotted two **huge spiderwebs** hanging from the beams of the ceiling. Obviously his grandma hadn't been up here in a while, or she would have cleaned things up. She was always cleaning something.

George didn't blame his grandma for not wanting to go up to the dusty and

gloomy attic. **It smelled really funky.** Like mothballs and old shoes.

And it was dark. The only thing lighting the room was a bare bulb in the middle of the ceiling. It cast some really **eerie shadows** on the wall. The sooner George could get out, the better!

He quickly walked over to the big old trunk in the corner of the attic.

"Whoa!" George exclaimed as he **bumped** into a lady standing in the shadows of the attic.

Huh? A lady in the attic?

Hey, where did *she* come from?

The lady didn't say. She couldn't. She had no mouth. Or arms. Or legs.

The lady was really an old dress mannequin his grandmother had stored up in the attic.

There was no one else there. Just George, the **creepy mannequin**, and the two spiders spinning their webs.

Actually, that wasn't exactly true.
There was **someone else**, in the attic. Well,
some*thing* else, anyway.

Something big and bubbly.

Something that bounced up and down and
all around.

The magical super burp was back! And it
was ready to play.

The bubbles were parachuting from
George's pancreas and spinning around his
spine. They were traipsing along his tonsils and
trampolining on his tongue.

George shut his mouth tight, trying to keep
that burp from sneaking out.

But there was no way this belch was getting
squelched. The burp had never played around
in an attic before.

Zing-zong. Bing-bong!

The bubbles twisted between George's teeth
and grappled with his gums. And then . . .

B-U-U-U-R-P!

George let out a **giant burp**. A magical super burp.

Now that the burp was on the loose, George was going to have to do whatever the burp wanted. And what the burp wanted was to see what was inside that trunk!

George's hands reached over and opened the trunk. Dust from the lid flew up into the air and landed **right in George's nose**.

Aaachoooo! George's nose let out a **string of boogers**. George wanted to wipe his nose. He really did. But the burp didn't feel like wiping. It felt like grabbing. So

George's hands reached into the trunk and grabbed a big black top hat.

George placed the hat on his head. Then his hands dived back into the trunk and pulled out **a flowing feather boa**, and wrapped it around his neck.

Suddenly, George's feet started moving—all on their own. One . . . two . . . cha-cha-cha. One . . . two . . . cha-cha-cha.

George didn't want his feet to move. He wanted to search the trunk for something he could use for his presentation. But George wasn't in charge anymore. The burp was. And the burp wanted to do **the cha-cha**!

George grabbed the mannequin and began twirling it around the dance floor . . . uh . . . er . . . *attic*.

One . . . two . . . cha-cha-cha. One . . . two . . . cha-cha-cha!

"What is going on up here?"

Suddenly, George heard his mother and his grandmother coming up the attic stairs. He wanted to whip off the boa, flip off the hat, and stop the dancing before they saw how **ridiculous** he looked. But the burp was having waaaayyy too much fun.

One . . . two . . . cha-cha-cha. One . . . two . . .

Pop! Suddenly George felt something burst in his belly. All the air rushed right out of him. The super burp was gone.

But George was still there. With a top hat on his head, a feather boa around his neck, a mannequin in his arms, and a **long string of boogers** hanging from his nose.

"Oh my goodness." George's mom laughed. "What were you doing?"

George opened his mouth to say "The cha-cha," and that's exactly what came out.

George's grandmother laughed.

"I'm glad you're having fun up here,

but it's almost dinnertime," George's
mom reminded him. "How about you
take off those things and start looking for
something you can use for your report?"

His grandmother handed him **a
tissue** from her pocket. "And wipe your
nose," she added.

George took the tissue
and **wiped**. Then he started
looking through the trunk.
There was nothing
special about most of
the stuff in there. Most
of it was just junk—
hats, shoes, and
some old books.

Suddenly, one
of the books caught
his eye. It was **bright
orange** with a **giant royal-looking seal**
stamped on the cover.

George flipped
the book open and
read a little. "Yes!" he
exclaimed. "This is
exactly what I need."

George started to show the book to
his mom and grandma. But then, he felt
something **weird** in his belly.

Oh no! Not the burp. Not again!

Gurgle. Glurp. Gurgle.

Phew. That wasn't a burp. It was just **hunger pangs**.

This time.

But there could always be another time when George wouldn't be **so lucky**. And what if that time turned out to be Friday night?

Chapter 6

"A cookbook?" Alex asked George as they walked to school the next day. "That was the **only thing** that you found at your grandmother's house?"

"Not just any cookbook," George corrected him. "A cookbook filled with recipes created by the Arfendonian royal palace chef. I'm going to cook a traditional **Arfendonian dish** and serve it to everyone on Friday."

Alex thought about that. "That's a great idea," he said. "You can tell a lot about a country by what the people eat. It shows what kind of food they grow on their farms. And that shows you what kind of **weather and soil** they have, because certain vegetables grow in moist soil while others grow in drier land."

"Exactly what I was thinking," George said. Even though he hadn't been thinking that at all. He'd just been happy to come up with a fun presentation about Arfendonia. "How's your presentation coming?"

"I could use a favor," Alex told him.

"Anything you need," George said. And he meant it. He owed Alex big-time. After all, his best pal had been spending a lot of time helping George try to find a **cure** for the super burp.

Alex was the only other person who knew about George's burping troubles. George hadn't told Alex. Alex was just so smart that he'd **figured it out** all by himself. Lucky for George, Alex was a good friend. He hadn't told anyone about the burp. And he'd vowed to help George find the cure.

So far, nothing had worked. Not the **onion milk shakes**, nor the spicy ginger candies. Nothing. But if anyone could find a cure, it would be Alex.

"I want to try to hypnotize you," Alex explained to George. "I've been reading up on it. And I think I hypnotized my neighbor's dog Josie last night. But it's hard to tell with **a dog**. I need a human to experiment on."

"I'm your guy," George said. Then he stopped for a second. "You're not going to make me do anything that will get me in trouble, right?"

Alex shook his head. "No. And besides, I can snap you right out of it by **snapping my fingers**."

"Okay, then," George said.

"Let's go over by that huge tree in the corner of the yard," Alex suggested. "I don't want anyone to see us. It will give away my whole presentation."

As George followed Alex over to the big tree, he felt something funny in the

bottom of his belly. Only this time it wasn't bubbles. And it wasn't bouncing. It was more like **wiggly worms** creeping and crawling inside him. The same feeling George always got when he was nervous.

Hypnotism was scary. George trusted Alex, but he was just a kid. What if things went wrong? What if George couldn't come out of it? Ever?

George's hands started to get all **moist and sticky**. He shoved them in his pockets and tried to dry them off.

"Now just relax," Alex said as he stopped by the huge tree. "Clear your mind."

George took a deep breath. He tried to stop the swarms of worms from **creeping and crawling** inside him.

Alex pulled a watch out of his pocket. It was silver and hanging from a chain.

"Cool! Where'd you get that?" George asked.

"It's my grandfather's **pocket watch**," Alex said. "I borrowed it for my hypnotism practice."

"Is it really old?" George asked. "Does it still work?"

"Yes, and yes," Alex said.

"What time is it, anyway?" George asked. He was **stalling** now. Maybe the bell would ring before Alex could try to hypnotize him.

"Eight twenty-three," Alex said. "Now stop asking questions. We don't have much time."

George took a deep breath. "Okay," he said. "I'm ready."

Alex started swinging the watch back and forth in front of George's eyes. "Just keep your eyes on the watch," Alex said in a slow, quiet, calm voice. "**Block out** any other distractions."

George's eyes moved from side to side as he watched the shiny watch swinging.

"You are getting sleepy," Alex said. **"Very sleepy."**

George blinked his eyes.

"Now close your eyes," Alex said. "And begin to drift off."

George closed his eyes.

"All you can hear is the sound of my voice," Alex told him.

But that wasn't true. He heard kids on the playground shouting. And the birds in the tree tweeting. And a couple of **squirrels chattering**.

"Here is my command," Alex continued. "Whenever you hear a buzzer sound, you will act like a monkey. And you will keep acting like a monkey until I snap my fingers. Now on the count of three, you will wake up. And you won't remember a thing about this hypnotism session."

But George knew he would remember. He **wasn't hypnotized** at all.

"One, two, three!" Alex said. "You can open your eyes now."

George opened his eyes.

"How do you feel?" Alex asked him.

"No different," George said. "I wasn't really asleep. I heard everything. And I remember everything."

BUZZZZZ. Just then the school buzzer rang. George did not act like a monkey.

Alex frowned. "I don't know where I went wrong," he said. He reached into his backpack, pulled out his book on hypnotism, and started to read as he walked.

George had seen Alex walk and read at the same time before. He always wondered how his best pal kept from bumping into things.

"Hey, Louie, whatcha doin'?" George heard Mike call out to Louie. Then he heard Max and Mike start **laughing hysterically**.

George didn't turn around to find out what was so funny. The less he had to look at Louie, the better.

"Hey Louie, that's hilarious!" Mike said.

"You look just like George when he went all crazy in class the other day," Max added.

That did it. George had to turn around now. And he didn't like what he saw.

Louie was goofing around, **scratching at his armpits**. Just like the burp had made George do on Monday morning.

What a jerk.

George turned to Alex. "Why does Louie hate me so much?" he asked.

Alex didn't answer. He was too busy reading his book to pay attention to Louie, or even to George.

"Hypnotism is much harder than I thought," Alex muttered to himself.

"I figured I would get it just like that."
He **snapped his fingers** in the air.

Just then, Louie stopped scratching.
He **glared** at George. "What are you
staring at?" he demanded.

"I wasn't staring," George told him.
Even though he was.

"That was the best George imitation
I've ever seen," Max told Louie.

"Yeah," Mike said. "You scratched
your pits just like him."

Louie gave Mike and Max a strange
look. "You guys are weird," he said. Then
he smiled. "But not as weird as **King
George** over there."

George sighed. He had a feeling King
George was going to be what Louie called
him from now on.

It sure would be great if Alex could
get this hypnotism thing working. Then
maybe he could hypnotize Louie into

being something **a little more human**.

Nah. It would take a lot more than just a pocket watch and a few words to do something like that. It would take a miracle.

Chapter 7

"I'm sure you'll be able to **hypnotize someone** at the assembly," George assured Alex that afternoon as the boys walked home from school. "You were probably doing it right. Maybe I'm just one of those people who can't be hypnotized."

"The book I checked out of the library did say that some people weren't susceptible to the **power of suggestion**," Alex agreed.

"Huh?" George asked.

"Some people can't be hypnotized," Alex explained. "You might be one of them."

"It's too bad," George said. "If I could be hypnotized, then you could hypnotize **the burp** right out of me." He frowned. "I really wish you could. Because if I burp up on that stage on Friday, it'll be a disaster. Don't you remember what happened when we went to see Mrs. Kelly perform on that dance show? The burp made me **dance my pants off** in front of a whole studio audience!"

"That one was hard to forget," Alex agreed.

"I'll say," George said. "I was dancing in my **tighty whities** in front of all those people. I can't let the burp do that to me again."

"It *would* be great if I could hypnotize

you not to burp," Alex said. He thought for a minute. "Of course, there might be another way to get rid of your burp."

"I'll try anything," George said.

Alex waved his arms. "Come on, we have to stop at Bartholomew's Bagels."

"I was kind of thinking I'd get **pizza** for a snack," George said.

"No, you want an everything bagel," Alex told him. "Trust me."

"Why?" George asked.

"Because **everything bagels** are covered in onions, garlic, salt, sesame seeds, and *caraway seeds*. The caraway seeds absorb gas in your stomach," Alex explained. "I read all about it on The Burp No More Blog. Some lady said she ate nothing but caraway seeds for **a whole day** and she stopped burping."

"I don't want to eat nothing but seeds." George groaned.

"That's why you're getting them on a bagel," Alex pointed out.

"I do like bagels," George agreed. He looked through the bagel-shop window and frowned. "But Louie and his Echoes are in there."

Alex laughed. He and George always called Max and Mike Louie's Echoes, because they repeated or agreed with **everything Louie said**.

Alex looked through the window. "What's Louie doing?" he asked, surprised.

George frowned. Louie was **scratching at his pits**, and jumping up and down. Again. And Max and Mike were laughing hysterically. Again.

"The same thing he always does," George said. "**Making fun of me.** Let's go somewhere else."

"You can't let Louie keep you from a

burp cure," Alex insisted.

"I guess not," George agreed. He pushed open the door to the bagel store. The buzzer rang, letting Mr. Bartholomew know that a customer had entered his shop.

Alex and George didn't even get through the doorway before they heard Mr. Bartholomew scolding Louie.

"Stop clowning around," Mr. Bartholomew told him. "Do you want a bagel or not?"

Louie smiled really wide so all his teeth showed.

"Oh no, here it comes," George grumbled. "He's gonna call me King George. **Or something worse.**"

Louie turned to George. He opened his mouth and said, "Ook, ook, ook."

"Huh?" George wondered.

"Ook, ook, ook." Louie bent over and started scratching his pits.

"Louie, I told you to stop," Mr. Bartholomew warned. "I don't know what's gotten into you. You started **going crazy** the minute you walked in here."

"Ook, ook!" Louie shouted. He started jumping up and down.

George looked at Alex. Alex stared back at George.

"That door buzzer," said Alex, thinking out loud. "Do you think—"

"He must have been **spying** on us before school," George concluded. Then he smiled. "Louie wasn't imitating me at all this morning. He was acting **all ape** because—"

"He was hypnotized!" Alex said. He was so excited he could barely speak. His voice came out in a whisper. "Louie turned into a monkey the minute he heard the buzzer on Mr. Bartholomew's door."

"Ook! Ook!" Louie scratched harder. He jumped higher.

"Louie! Stop that!" Mr. Bartholomew shouted. "This is a bagel shop, **not a zoo**."

"Ook! Ook!" Louie ooked back.

"I'm sorry, but you have to leave," Mr. Bartholomew said. "I can't have kids monkeying around in here."

Louie leaped toward the door and pushed Alex and George out of the way. He scratched happily at **his pits** and smiled as he ran away. "Ook, ook!"

"Hey, wait for me!" Mike shouted as he ran after Louie.

"And me!" Max added. He ran out after Louie, too.

"I gotta snap Louie **out of this**," Alex said.

George laughed. "Why? I think it's hilarious."

"Come on." Alex grabbed George and pulled him out of the bagel store.

"Doesn't anyone want **a bagel**?" Mr. Bartholomew asked as the door shut.

"Louie! Wait up!" Alex shouted.

"I can help you."

Louie turned around and bared his teeth. "Ook, ook!"

Alex ran to catch up with Louie. And then . . . snap! Alex snapped his fingers.

Louie **stopped** scratching. And leaping. And ook-ooking.

Louie looked around. "How'd I get out here?" he asked.

"That was funny, Louie," Max told him.

"**Really funny**," Mike said. "I was laughing so hard."

"I was laughing harder," Max insisted.

"What are you guys talking about?" Louie demanded.

"How you went all ape in the bagel store," Max said. "You were great."

"A great ape," Mike agreed.

Louie stared at them **blankly**. Then he looked over at Alex and George.

"What are you two doing here?" he demanded.

"We followed you out of the bagel shop," George said. "Because Alex is the only one who can help you."

"Help me?" Louie said. "I'm not the one who needs help. It's you who needs help. Especially if you think I'm gonna let you hang out with me. I don't want to be seen anywhere near a **royal jerk** like you, *King George*."

"Louie, the thing is, when you were spying on us today, you—" Alex began.

"Spying?" Louie shouted. "What makes you think I was spying on you?"

"The fact that you **turned into a monkey** when that buzzer rang in the bagel shop," George said.

"I didn't do that," Louie insisted. "And I would never spy on you, George. You're not that interesting." He turned to Mike and Max. "Let's get out of here. I don't want a bagel, anyway. For some reason, I'm in the mood for a **banana split**."

Louie turned and walked away. Max and Mike followed close behind.

"But, Louie—" Alex began.

But George stopped him. "Forget it," he said. "He doesn't deserve your help."

"I guess not," Alex said. "You want to go get that everything bagel now?"

"Sure." George smiled. He was glad Mr. Bartholomew wasn't going to be mad at him when he got there. This time someone else had **gotten in trouble**. That felt good

And the fact that it had been Louie who had gone all crazy in there made it even better.

Chapter 8

"Okay, George," his mom said as they walked into the supermarket that evening. "I'm going to pick up a few things for dinner in the produce section while you get the **ingredients** you need to make your Arfendonian special."

"I've got my list right here," George said, holding up a sheet of paper. "This is going to be the **best report** of the whole night."

"It will be different," his mom agreed. "Just go get your ingredients and meet me at the cash register. And don't get into any trouble, okay?"

"Okay." George wasn't worried. He'd eaten two of Mr. Bartholomew's everything bagels. That meant he'd had a lot of caraway seeds. If Alex was right, this time the burp would **stay away**.

George began looking up and down the aisle for the first item on his list. Suddenly, he felt something else going up and down. Up and down . . . *and all around*. Bubbles! **Hundreds of them!** And they were all in his belly.

Oh no. Not right after he'd promised his mom he would stay out of trouble.

George had to keep that burp from bursting out of him. Maybe if he **held his breath**, there wouldn't be enough air to keep the bubbles alive.

He shut his mouth tight and **pinched his nose shut**.

But this burp wasn't going to be kept down. Already it was leaping over his lungs and speeding across his scapula.

George was **turning blue** from holding his breath.

The bubbles moved into his mouth. They licked at his lips.

The room was **spinning**. George needed air. He couldn't keep from breathing another minute. He just had to . . .

The minute George opened his mouth to breathe, the burp burst out. And now whatever the burp wanted to do, George had to do.

The burp was **hungry**. Really, *really* hungry. It wanted to eat.

George's hands started tearing at a big box of Crunch Munchies cereal— which was strange, because it wasn't breakfast time. It was almost dinnertime! But burps don't care about things like that.

Crunch! Crunch! Crunch!

The **Crunchy Munchies** were sweet. But they were also dry. What they needed was milk.

George's feet started running toward the dairy case. His hands grabbed a container of milk and started pouring **cold, creamy milk** down his throat. *Gulp. Gulp. Gulp.*

"Young man!" one of the grocers shouted. "Stop that right now!"

George wanted to stop. He really did. But George wasn't in charge. The burp was. And it was in the mood for a **chocolaty dessert**.

George hurried past the canned soups and the pasta. He leaped through the cleaning products and the paper towels.

"Hey! Slow down!" shouted a woman standing near a big display of **toilet-paper rolls**.

George didn't slow down. He couldn't. The burp wouldn't let him.

The woman jumped out of George's way—and *BAM!* She landed in the middle of all those toilet-paper rolls. They **fell to the floor** in a heap!

The grocer raced
around the corner. "Stop!" he
shouted at George. "You . . ."

Whoops! The grocer tripped
over a package of toilet paper. He landed
right on his **rear end**. *Thud!*

"Cut it out!" the grocer yelled at
George. "You've caused enough trouble."

But the burp didn't think that was
true. It still had much more trouble to

cause. So George kept running.

George stopped in front of a big **ice-cream** freezer. His hands grabbed a tub of chocolate ice cream and ripped off the lid. George dug one of his hands into the tub and scooped out a big blob of frozen chocolaty goodness. He **shoved the handful** of ice cream into his mouth.

"Yummy!" George's mouth exclaimed.

His whole body began wiggling, jiggling, and shaking all around.

Wiggle wiggle. Jiggle jiggle. Shake.

Just then, George's mother raced down the aisle. "George! What do you think you're doing?" she demanded.

"Making a **chocolate shake**!" George answered. That wasn't what George had wanted to say. But George wasn't in charge of his mouth anymore. The super burp was.

George took **another handful** of ice

cream and shoved it in his mouth. Then
he started shaking again.

*Wiggle wiggle. Jiggle
jiggle. Shake . . . Pop!*

George felt
something burst in the
bottom of his belly. All
the air rushed out of
him.

The magical
super burp was gone.
But George was still
there—with a **milk
mustache** and a
chocolate ice-cream beard.

"What do you have to say for
yourself?" his mother yelled.

George opened his mouth to say "I'm
sorry." And that's exactly what came out.

The grocer came hurrying. He was
rubbing his aching rear end with one

hand, and holding a mop with the other.

"Clean up in aisle four," he told George as he handed him the mop. "And aisle six. And aisle eight. **Get moving.**"

George started mopping. What else could he do?

At least this time, the burp had left a mess that *could* be cleaned up. Once George finished, there wouldn't be any evidence that it had caused trouble at all.

But if the burp came again tomorrow at the Family Tree Festival Assembly, there would be **news cameras** there to record the whole thing. Evidence that would last forever.

That would be *really* bad!

Chapter 9

"I'm nervous," Alex told George on Friday night. "I've never hypnotized anyone in front of a **big crowd** before."

George sat down in the front row of the auditorium beside his best buddy and frowned. "*You're* nervous?" he asked. "What about me? What if the you-know-what slips out on TV?"

Before Alex could answer, Louie came **strolling down the aisle**. He was wearing a big top hat and a red-and-white-striped jacket.

"Who are you supposed to be?" Alex asked him.

"It's a surprise," Louie said. He glared

at George. "But I'll tell you one thing. It's a lot cooler than being a relative of a **make-believe king** from a pretend country."

"King Stanley is not make-believe," George told him. "Arfendonia is a real place."

"No one is going to believe that," Louie replied. "You're going to make a fool of yourself."

George gulped. That was completely possible.

Mrs. Kelly climbed up onto the stage. Instantly, the auditorium quieted down.

"I'd like to welcome all of you to Edith B. Sugarman Elementary's Fourth-Grade Family Tree Festival Assembly," the teacher said. She pointed to the side of the stage where a news reporter and a cameraman were standing. "With a **special welcome** to the news team from

Beaver Brook's own Channel Forty-Seven."

Everyone in the auditorium applauded. The **news reporter** smiled and held up her microphone.

"And now," Mrs. Kelly said, "we will hear from our first student, Louie Farley."

Louie walked up onto the stage. In a **very loud voice**, he announced, "Ladies and gentlemen. Children of all ages. Turn

your attention to the center ring."

George was surprised. Louie sounded like a **circus ringmaster**.

"Most of the members of my family have been successful lawyers," Louie said. "*Very* successful."

George rolled his eyes and yawned. No surprise there.

"But when I did my research, I discovered that I had a relative who had a very different job," Louie continued. "My great-great-grandfather Petey Farley was a show-business star. He worked at the Jingling Sisters Circus!"

George sat back up. That was actually **pretty cool**.

"Great-Great-Grandfather Petey was responsible for the upkeep of the center ring," Louie continued. "That's the most important ring. Only **the stars** of the circus perform there."

Louie started to bow and end his presentation, but Mrs. Kelly stopped him. "What was your great-great-grandfather's **official title**, Louie?" she asked.

Louie crinkled his forehead. He took a deep breath. Finally, he said, "I couldn't find the exact title, but my mom told me that it would probably have been something like Chief Large Animal Waste Disposal Engineer."

George thought about that for a minute. Then he whispered to Alex, "Does that mean Louie's great-great-grandfather scooped up **circus elephant poop**?"

Suddenly all the kids in the front rows started laughing. Which made the adults start to laugh. Soon, even the TV

cameraman was laughing.

Louie turned bright red. For a minute, George thought **he might cry**.

George felt rotten. He hadn't meant to say that so loud. He was just excited that he had figured it out, and it **slipped out** of his mouth. He really hadn't meant to make Louie feel like a jerk onstage. He wouldn't do that to anyone. Not even Louie.

"That's a very important job, Louie," Mrs. Kelly said loudly.

The audience grew quiet. Everyone wanted to hear why Mrs. Kelly thought **poop scooping** was so important.

"Your great-great-grandfather was part of a legacy of circus folk who made sure the animals were kept clean and healthy," Mrs. Kelly explained. "You should be proud."

Louie stood a little taller. He smiled.

Buzz . . . Buzz . . .

Just then the cell phone of one of the parents began **buzzing** in the audience. She turned it off quickly. But not quick enough, because . . .

Suddenly Louie bent over. He scratched his head and started leaping up and down.

"Ook! Ook! Ook!" he shouted.

"Uh-oh," Alex said.

Mrs. Kelly began to laugh. "What a wonderful imitation of one of your great-great-grandfather's **beloved animals**!" she exclaimed.

"Ook! Ook! Ook!" Louie replied.

The audience applauded.

"That's my son!" Ms. Farley said loud enough for the **entire audience** to hear.

"Make sure you get a good shot of this," the news reporter told her cameraman.

Louie scratched his pits. He jumped up and down. **He bared his teeth.**

"You hypnotized him big-time," George told Alex. "He looks like an angry monkey."

"Do you know what **monkeys** do when they get angry?" Alex asked George nervously.

"No," George said. "What?"

"**They throw their poop,**" Alex said.

George gulped. He figured he'd be the first one Louie aimed at.

"What are you waiting for?" George asked Alex. "Get up there and stop this!"

Alex leaped up onstage. He stood next to Louie and snapped his fingers. Hard.

Snap!

Louie stopped scratching, jumping, and ooking. He looked out blankly into the audience.

"What is going on here?" Mrs. Farley demanded. She came running down the aisle toward the stage. "Alex, what did you do to my **Loo Loo Poo**?"

Everyone in the audience started to laugh, again. Louie turned bright red, again. "Mom!" he shouted. "I told you not to call me that."

"I hypnotized him," Alex explained.

The audience **stopped laughing**. They stared at Alex.

"Why would you do that?" Mrs. Kelly asked him.

"I didn't mean to," Alex told her. "I was trying to hypnotize George. Louie was **spying on us** from behind a tree. I guess he got hypnotized instead."

"I wasn't spying on you," Louie insisted.

"Then how come you got hypnotized?" Alex asked him.

Louie didn't answer.

"Why were you hypnotizing *anybody*?" Mrs. Kelly asked.

"I was **practicing** for my presentation," Alex explained. "My great-uncle Samuel was a hypnotist."

The cameraman pointed his camera away from Louie and focused it on Alex.

"I think Louie's behavior has proven that you've **mastered that skill**," Mrs. Kelly said. "Great job."

"I don't think it's so great," Louie insisted. "I don't want to keep turning into a monkey every time I hear a buzzer."

"You won't," Alex promised him. "Hypnotism wears off. You're probably going to be fine in a day or two. Just **stay away** from buzzers until then."

That didn't seem to make Louie any happier.

Mrs. Kelly smiled at Alex. "Since you're up here already," she told him, "why don't you go next? I think we are all now **very interested** in hypnotism."

The audience applauded. George stuck his fingers in his mouth and whistled.

"You should thank my Loo Loo Poo,"

Mrs. Farley shouted to Alex. "After all, he was the one who got himself hypnotized. He's the *real* star of your presentation."

"Um . . . thank you, Loo Loo Poo," Alex said.

The audience started laughing.

Louie's face turned **bright red**. He was really, really angry. Angrier than George had ever seen him.

It was a good thing Alex was there to snap his fingers and snap Louie out of acting like a monkey. Otherwise, the whole auditorium could be covered with **flying angry Loo Loo *Poop*!**

Chapter 10

George wiggled to the right. He wiggled to the left. **He twiddled his thumbs.** The presentations were going on and on. And George hadn't had his turn yet. It wasn't easy, sitting still waiting. This was the longest assembly ever.

Sure, it had been fun watching Alex hypnotize the news reporter into thinking she was **a pigeon** that cooed and flapped her wings.

And seeing Sage hold a snake had been pretty cool—until she dropped it and everyone realized it was **rubber**.

But George was getting antsy.

He couldn't wait for everyone to know about his relation to King Stanley of Arfendonian. And to have a taste of real Arfendonian food.

Not that George had tasted it yet, either. There hadn't been time. The treat was **still warm** from the oven when he'd thrown it into the plastic container and jumped into the car to come to the presentation.

But he was sure it had to be delicious. After all, **the recipe** had been created by the royal chef of Arfendonia.

"And now, we will hear from George Brown," Mrs. Kelly announced.

George jumped at the sound of his name. Quickly he popped a **paper crown** onto his head and picked up his food container.

"My research led me to a small island nation in the North Atlantic Ocean,"

George began as he stepped up to the microphone. "It is such a small country that most people haven't heard of it. **I sure hadn't.** Most maps don't even include it. But my relatives come from this place—including His Majesty, King Stanley of Arfendonia, who is my **seventeenth cousin twice removed** on my mother's side."

Everyone in the audience started talking at once.

"That's so cool," George heard someone say.

"A king," someone else added. "Amazing!"

"Well," the news reporter said into the camera, "it appears we have a royal family right here in Beaver Brook!"

The cameraman on the side of the stage pointed his camera at George for **a close-up**.

George smiled. Louie had been wrong. People did believe in Arfendonia. And they believed that King Stanley was George's cousin. Well, his seventeenth cousin twice removed, anyway.

George held up his food container. "This is a traditional Arfendonian meal," he told everyone. "A blue cheese, anchovy, macaroni, garlic, and **chopped tongue** casserole. I brought plates and forks so anyone who wants to can have a taste."

George whipped the top off his food container. The smell of baked stinky cheese, **hairy fish**, and meat that had once been in the mouth of a cow filled the auditorium.

"P.U.!" Louie shouted. He held his

nose. "**That stinks.** I gotta get out of here." He ran up the aisle toward the door.

"Right behind you, Louie," Max called.

"No, *I'm* right behind you," Mike shouted. He pushed his way past Max.

"Sorry, dude," Alex called to George as he ran up the aisle. "But that stuff **smells awful**. I can't breathe."

Everyone was leaving. Even George's own mom and dad.

The news reporter and cameraman raced off the stage and started to follow the crowd.

"Wait," George called. "I'm sure it **tastes better** than it smells."

The news reporter looked up at the stage. "You haven't tried it?" she asked, surprised.

"I didn't have time," George said. "But it's a favorite of the Arfendonian royal family, and I'm a member of that family. So I'm sure I'll like it."

The news reporter pinched her nose. "Let's see about that," she said.

George took a **heaping helping** of casserole and popped it into his mouth.

Actually, it wasn't so bad. Maybe you had to have actual Arfendonian blood running through you to appreciate it.

But then . . .

Something else starting running through George's body. **Something wiggly.** And jiggly. It was heading up his throat. And into his mouth. And then . . .

BAAARRRFFFF!

George puked. Threw up. Hurled. Spewed. Blew his lunch. Tossed his cookies.

The news reporter sure didn't want to get that on camera. She and the cameraman raced out of the auditorium holding their noses.

Now everyone was gone. Except for George. He was still there, **covered in barf**, and holding a blue cheese, anchovy, macaroni, garlic, and tongue casserole. Yuck.

George had a feeling his mom and dad weren't going to let him get in the car stinking like *that*. Which meant the seventeenth cousin twice removed from the king of Arfendonia would be walking home through town **smelling** like barfendonia.

George sniffed the air around him. The anchovies, tongue, and cheese smelled **pretty ripe** now. Which proved one thing: There actually was something worse than a magical super burp—a king-size Arfendonian barf!

Chapter 11

"Hey, Mom, I'm home!" George called as he ran into his house after school, about a week after the family-tree presentations.

"Hi honey," George's mom said as she came to greet him. She held out a large, **cream-colored envelope**. "This came for you this morning."

"Mail? For me?" George asked excitedly. "Who's it from?"

"Open it and see," his mother replied.

George looked at the envelope. "Hey, isn't that the same seal as the one on the cover of **the cookbook** Grandma gave me?"

George's mom nodded. "Yep. It's the royal seal of Arfendonia."

George **tore open** the envelope and pulled out a thick piece of paper.

Dear Cousin George,

A

One of my royal subjects has brought to my attention that you recently appeared on an American television special and spoke about your Arfendonian roots. I was quite excited to hear about another member of our royal family.

I was especially impressed to hear that you had prepared our traditional casserole. You must be very brave. No one in our family has ever eaten the casserole. We have always insisted our royal tasters try it first— and none of them have ever been able to keep it down.

I look forward to meeting you, my courageous cousin—the 1,214th person in line to become king of Arfendonia.

All the best,
His Majesty, King Stanley of Arfendonia

Just then, George smelled something coming from the kitchen. It stank like **dirty socks and vinegar**.

"What is that?" he asked his mom.

"Cabbage and brussels sprout soup," she said. "I'm trying a new recipe from the Arfendonian cookbook."

George frowned. Now he wished he wasn't so far down on the list of people to become king of Arfendonia. Because kings had **royal tasters** to try the food before they did. And George sure could use one of those now.

Or better yet, how about a royal **burper**! Someone to burp instead of George. Someone else to get in trouble for a change.

Now *that* would really come in handy!

About the Author

Nancy Krulik is the author of more than 150 books for children and young adults, including three *New York Times* Best Sellers and the popular Katie Kazoo, Switcheroo books. She lives in New York City with her family, and many of George Brown's escapades are based on things her own kids have done. (No one delivers a good burp quite like Nancy's son, Ian!) Nancy's favorite thing to do is laugh, which comes in pretty handy when you're trying to write funny books! You can follow Nancy on Twitter: @NancyKrulik.

About the Illustrator

Aaron Blecha was raised by a school of giant squid in Wisconsin and now lives with his family by the south English seaside. He works as an artist designing funny characters and illustrating humorous books, including the one you're holding. You can enjoy more of his weird creations at www.monstersquid.com.